the shingle weaver's journal

the Shingle Weaver's Journal

poems by
Carlos Reyes

LHP

ACKNOWLEDGMENTS

Some of these poems first appeared in *The Human Voice Quarterly, Kayak, Litmus, Local Earth, Matrix, Mojo Navigator, One Mind, The Oregonian, The Other Side, Out of Sight Library, Poet Lore, The Portland Review, Potpourri, Roots Forming, Sand Castles, The,* and *The Willamette Bridge.*

In addition:

"Cutting Shake Bolts on the East Fork" and "Oregon Ash" appeared in *Shake/Bolts* (Milwaukee: Monday Morning Press, 1972).

"Trask River" and "For A Mountain Girl" appeared in *The Windows* (Canada: Weed/flower Press, 1966; 1967).

"To Watch Ships" appeared in *Action In The North Atlantic* (Portland: Another Press, 1971).

"Why Laughter Is Not Always The Best Medicine" was included in *The Prisoner* (Santa Barbara: Capra, 1971).

The author wishes to express special thanks to Bill Benton, Christopher Howell, and Phil Garrison for their help in assembling this book.

Typography & design by Maggie Checkoway Howell.

Cover photograph by Karen Stoner Reyes.

The publication of this book was made possible in part through a grant from the National Endowment for the Arts, a federal agency.

Library of Congress Cataloging in Publication Data

Reyes, Carlos.
The shingle weaver's journal.

I. Title.
PS3568.E883S5 811'.54 80-16387
ISBN 0-89924-027-5

Printed by John Laursen at Press-22, Portland, Oregon, USA.
First Edition.

Lynx House Press • Box 800 • Amherst, Massachusetts 01004

For Karen

I. LOOK FOR ME

Scapulamancie	3
Red Foxes	5
In Cupped Hands	6
3 Women In The Woods	7
For George & His Kayak	8
The Way A Ship Slides Down	9
The Dream	10
Poem For The Bride Of Atahualpa	11
To Watch Ships	13
Poem For Nina Heloise	14
Why Laughter Is Not Always The Best Medicine	15
Passage	16

II. IN DEFENSE

Salt	21
Maine	22
Twelve Degrees North Of The Equator	23
Black Mystique	24
Under The Freeway	25
Two For Pablo	26
The Fight, The Dance, The Tribute	27
The Caves Along The Osage	28
Kansas: Eighty Years Later	30
Numbers	31
The Angel	32
Something Is Lost In Translation, Almost Always	33
Let Me Count The Ways	34
Masks On J-Street	36
And See If Anybody Salutes	37

III. THE SHINGLE WEAVER'S JOURNAL

Pyrite	41
The Shingle Weaver	42
Grindstone Mtn	43
Cedar Butte Lookout: 1953	44
For A Mountain Girl	45
Crabbing At Netarts	46
Cutting Shake-Bolts On The East Fork	47
Four Thirty P.M.	48
Tupper	49
The Blacksmith Shop At St Luke	51
1947	52
Are You Sure You Are Lying To Me?	53
Trask River	54
The Valley By Trask House	55
The Knot	56
Ghosts	59
Caulk Boots	61
Shattering Of A Myth	62
I Feel Like	63
Oregon Ash	64
The Bark Shanty	65
The Shingle Weaver's Journal	66

I.

Look For Me

Look for me at the end
of the red road; don't try

to count the white
crosses along the black road;

turn left after you
pass the colorblind intersection;

meet me where
the two clouds cross

SCAPULAMANCIE

I

He looks at his hands
small for a man
of his size

the rivers there
go nowhere

begin are lost
on the same plain

a poor map
with which to start
the journey his feet
are too small

The fog moves in
on him
like a blanket
left out to air and
dry then rained on

How he longed
to be away

II

Ridges and valleys
a kind of scapulamancie
(without the scapula) the
game played

solitaire
as he sits on the
cedar

logs and counts
the ridges on
the fingers of both

hands: ten ridges, ten
valleys thinking
about the journey
about what lay
beyond the ten

ridges imagining thirty people
with sixty hands
a forest of snags

the sea fog spilling over

RED FOXES

Up along the fence
row near the edge of
the fir grove stand
two red foxes   we
suppose because of
the distance one is
male the other female
they appear in the
pasture hesitant
as they eye the tract
homes below and west
go back into the woods

We stand you and I
in the back yard
behind the old house
certain that they
can see us   the two
red foxes thinking
they know what we are
thinking as we watch
them and they watch us

IN CUPPED HANDS

I walk along the beach, alone
in the night and blowing sand.
This afternoon I did not wade in the surf
but stayed back as though the sea
were shut off from me by the sand
and the drift log. We built a fire
behind the log and spent a lot of time there
trying to avoid the rain and smoke.
You went back to the cabin. I stayed.
Leaning hard on the log I watched
the waves coming in and could not
be drawn out, but stayed inside, protected.
This morning growing in the sand
I found a funny wild flower. I
pulled it up and brought it to you
offering it in cupped hands.

3 WOMEN IN THE WOODS

In the first woods she was coming towards
me through the fog and fir trees
the woman waved from a distance in the second
as oak trees shed their leaves

I was there alone wondering why she was not
with me
the room was as empty as I
disappeared from my own view in the painting

The moon was full in the third
woods here
was no woman
and trees on the high plateau

FOR GEORGE & HIS KAYAK

The kayak is made from the skin
of an anaconda, the ribs
bleached in the Mojave
of various small animals;
the wishbone of a pterodactyl
when broken in half
will make a fine pair of oars.
He will sit amidships
on his knees
the scapula of a kodiak
bear on which he sees a map
of the world he travels through.

THE WAY A SHIP SLIDES DOWN

Some one forgot
the champagne, brought
instead polluted water
from the Willamette
There is no arm strong
enough to break the coke
bottle and the bow
crumples like balsa
under the impact
The Captain is some where
else drunk in Valhalla
a tavern on Burnside Street
where he has shanghied
a crew from among the winos
The charts in his back
pockets are written
in classic transylvanian & crushed
between his tremendous ass
and the oak bar stool
Thursday he sobers
up a coast guard captain will come
and tell him his ship
has been launched and floats
free, last reported
five hundred miles South
West of Cape Blanco
& drifting

The trees would not stop after the seven hills
where the smokey purple ridges are stacked up
one behind the other and you could count them
until your eyes grew tired and between each
was a valley and a river, and maybe a meadow
where the widest road was a deer trail
a few inches wide and a thousand miles long
and where what you thought was smoke
from a cabin or a mill was morning mist rising
and where what you thought was smoke
from a cannon
was morning mist

POEM FOR THE BRIDE OF ATAHUALPA

—the wall
one's up against
the flesh turned to stone
—Robert Creeley, *St. Martins*

Sun rise
one ray of sun
light
strikes her
tinder, starts
the fire
she dances
as a wisp
smoke in the wet wood

The sun goes
the moon comes
the woods are stone
as she is a stone
—a cold stone
bleeding
against your heart

The ring
swirls a
round
the knot

torture of wood
caught is the
agatized dance
still movement
agonized
in what once was
wood the sun
goes and comes
the moon and the stone
is cold
on your finger

TO WATCH SHIPS

Hammond, Oregon
June 10, 1969

Fools we came
here at 2 a.m.
standing on the ruins
of Ft Stevens, buried
in the sand to wait.
5 a.m. & it is up
this tricky channel, of
shifting bottom sands, the
way ships must come
from the sea
through the grave-
yard into the Columbia, up
to Portland (Hardly
before we were awake
small fishing boats slipped
silently passing
down the mist
into the Pacific
then dim light
ghosts come: destroyers
the destroyer escorts, the LST
one submarine
black, hard
silhouette passes
war (pale grey
ships go
past in a long quiet heart beat

POEM FOR NINA HELOISE

The Shoshone, on discovering his new child
is a daughter, walks down into the beautiful
valley where the seeds grow

I have walked that way four times in my life.
The first time after long hours of watching
and waiting, tired and disappointed I made that journey.
Once I came back in a slow falling rain. Another time
I walked across the great desert to return to my house.
Finally, I went to that valley on a summer day
bright with sunshine and blue.

On the day my youngest daughter begins her menses
I will go to my doorway and shout the news to the village
and give away one of my horses to an old man

WHY LAUGHTER IS NOT ALWAYS THE BEST MEDICINE

"Tengo mucho miedo
de las hojas muertas"
—G. Lorca, *Aire de Nocturno*

October must be the death of all things
that I do not fear dying, but October.
It is not October that I fear, it is
what comes after: it is winter I fear.
Winter is truly the death of all things.

Today, the 26th of October, daylight saving
time ended and somewhere in the hour we lost
when we set the clock back was
the death of all things

I

Days.
Passing days
& nights passing
nights.
Ships in the night
as you went by
I waved, that
night
& wondered who
you were
& now, begin
to wonder if
you waved back
& if it's important
(the passing
  the waving
  the nights
  the days
  passing

II

As you came by
black & sleek
with running
lights missing
(there was no fog just
  black
ness.
You insisted there was no need
for lights.
I thought I saw a lamp
flickering in your state room (bed room?)
& will that
flame matter
when the ship collides
w/ something yet
undefined in the absolute
darkness

III

The water is deep enough
to drown in
(you can drown in a tea -cup
it is
said
the water is oily
propellers barely making
sound.
There is no one
at the bridge
there is no bridge
there is no ship

there is your lamp
flickering in the window
of the passing night

II.

In Defense

I offer a poem freshly killed,
a junky who would do anything,
a thief becoming a thief,
an adulterer going to bed,
a rapist going to rape,
an unnatural act about to begin,
a leech too fat to walk back to Akron,
my casket hand carved by me
from cheap pine and painted
with black Shinola.

SALT

Shoes worn, unpolished
clothes wrinkled stubble
beard over the wrinkled
map of the sea
of Burnside Street tokay

As though
kept put away in mothballs
saved for this occasion
the hat

sits square on his head
as he on the bench, new
First Engineer's cap; thick
embroidered felt design
above the bill bright gold
three bladed propeller

beneath the black
brim eyes, clouded
the sea, his dignity
from Goodwill
or Eddie's Loan & Pawn

Now, he holds his
two year old grandchild
feeding it orange juice
rocking it in his arms, the rhythm
unmistakable

MAINE

Uptown, at the barbershop
the pool has been formed:
each man has put in his
four bits and picked the day
the old car under the bridge
will fall through the ice.
The woolen mill at Old Town
has been struck for almost a year;
production is not curtailed
                                    —there is always
                                      someone who needs
work *Ice on the Stillwater is breaking up*
and the men of the village are busy
                                      building
                                      new bases
for the brass cannons
            that face
the river

TWELVE DEGREES NORTH OF THE EQUATOR

The morning is sweaty with a hangover.
Rubbing grains of sand from my eyes,
having spent all night underground
I squint at a dim sun through fog
hear for the first time monkeys
chattering, birds squawking and see
the first morning of the world.
A coatimundi is in the trash barrel
looking for food among the ashes
of classified documents

BLACK MYSTIQUE

Judy was black Judy
was an Amazon.
Judy liked to fight
liked to dance loved
loving beer
marijuana Judy
gave Jake the crabs.
Judy spent time
in jail one night
Judy took me home
to her bed and did not
give me crabs she kept
in her bra wheat
straw cigarette papers
and a razor
blade (Jake told me that
several days later

UNDER THE FREE WAY

Yesterday I saw a brown wrinkled
paper bag of a man walk

through four muscatel bottles
and come out clean shaven

TWO FOR PABLO

I

When I run out of blue
I use red, sd Picasso
which explains a lot
of things, say, for example
why the harlequin has
one blue ball, one red
but does not explain
that quizzical look
in Pablo's eyes as he
stares between his legs

II

A blue sun drops
behind forty miles of
smoke painted by Picasso
imagine that this is Portland,
Oregon. The forest is burning down
the last four lines are false
you have sneezed on your mustache
your last friend has just said
goodbye

THE FIGHT, THE DANCE, THE TRIBUTE

That yesterday I sneezed
on the sleeve of a man
who died today, this morning
disconcerting
that a child runs across
four lanes of traffic
against the light and does
a wild victory dance
on the other side, at noon

We walk tonight talking of other things
in our neighborhood a dog lies on the sidewalk
beside a busy thoroughfare
one cold eye is open
on his nose is a copper penny
making a pair with the other eye
we pass wide around it
as though afraid
that death has set a trap for us
baited it with that shiny penny
waits to bite the hand
that reaches out for it

THE CAVES ALONG THE OSAGE

Hidden entrances, where
hillsides open
into rooms of the
limestone caves

—often echoing
chambers & flowing
rivers beneath the earth
Saturdays we spend
exploring, in the dark

—brave in the stories
we tell the following
Monday

—we always carry a ball
of twine, short pieces of
string saved for months,
to unwind as we go in, so
we can find our way
out & candles to
light in the dark

—we can hear the rushing
water of the river, deep & wonder
about eyeless fish & we are
scared of snakes & the warmth/damp
ness & whatelse we do not know

—minutes of excitement
enough
for several days
later, of talk

—never bothering to mention
we never go far enough
to unwind the ball of twine;
that we never dare light the candles

KANSAS: EIGHTY SIX YEARS LATER

A streetcar up on blocks was home,
in a tourist court called Uncle Tom's
Cabins. On Saturday we went up town.
One night my father took me
to the auditorium. He pointed
and said: That's Joe Lewis
heavyweight champion of the world.
When I think of 1943, the war
and Salina, Kansas, I can see
the regiment of black soldiers
—strings broken on their white
leggings—marching up the road.

NUMBERS

1. The boy rolled down the grassy hill
   like the three thirty bell
   on the first day of school

2. The boy rolled down the slope
   like a ball the boy rolled down

3. the hill like an old woman
   rolling down her brown cotton stockings

4. The boy rolled down the hill like a boy

5. The boy rolled down his weathered cheek

THE ANGEL

I saw him sitting there
perched on the bead
at the end of the double
barreled 12 gauge shot
gun, a man in uniform
gave me that gun, brass
cased shells, told me to
fire two rounds into
a fifty gallon drum
when the first round went
off the angel was
clearly shaken a bit, but dancing
on top of the drum, when
the pellets struck
he was already gone, and I
was ready
to be a prison
chaser (I never saw him
again —or if I did, I didn't
recognize him among the
others & I was never willing
to do his time for him
& didn't want to kill
him for it

SOMETHING IS LOST IN TRANSLATION, ALMOST ALWAYS

They are writing on the cold blue
paper of the Pacific. Canada is beautiful
but I don't like the cold winter waters . . .

They are thinking of you and us . . .

Are you going with me or with him?

The lessons are especially difficult.

This one is mine; that one is his. The
house on the corner belongs to Jorge.

Our summer house is close to the sea.

LET ME COUNT THE WAYS

1. I love you like the bats that fly
   from caves

2. I love you like a 1950
   Crosley station wagon

3. I love you like an old man
   who stumps down the street on his peg leg
   hand carved from hickory

4. I love you like Yankee Doodle Dandy
   played on a calypso drum
   made from a milk can

5. I love you like a ringing phone
   at 2 a.m.
   hung up at the other end
   before I answer

6. I love you like a round
   trip ticket
   to Empire, Oregon

7. I love you like a boot-legger
   in modern day Wichita

8. I love you like a bat hanging
   up side down
   in a plastic milk carton
   dreaming of sudden freedom in Carlsbad

9. I love you like a tune lost
in the vastness of a bushel

10. I love you like flat beer
used
to kill slugs on the lawn

11. I love you the way
a ship slides down

12. I love you like what's left
of the world

MASKS ON J-STREET

Panama: 1955

Rodriquez, the Mexican who couldn't speak
Spanish, he said. And Roger the Cherokee
who had to fight to prove he wasn't
a Panamanian. & Clutch Riley, the Texan, telling
Preston, Man, it don't make no difference
when you go home on leave, you see my folks
you hear? & Bob Young who married the Cuban
singer, dancer and bar girl
in spite of the objections of the C.O. and the Rabbi.
& Preston whispering to me he's going
down to Chorrillo where *he* can find a woman, that I'd
better stay here with Riley and the others.
& Rico, the West Indian bartender, toeing the mark
for his bosses. & Cholo, full-blooded
Choco Indian, mopping up the floor.
& the bar maids inside the bar
& the blue mooners at the tables
& the whores in the street
& the fairy waiting in the shadows
whispering at passing G. I. s
& Clutch Riley saying to Preston
Man, it don't make no difference . . .

AND SEE IF ANYBODY SALUTES

My poetry is railroad tracks,
tall fir trees standing
or falling as I stand
chain saw in hand.

My poetry is the truck
I don't drive
and tall tales told
me beside the old times.

My poetry is that.
Language. And languages
of monarch butterflies migrating from Panama
to Panama.

III.

The Shingle Weaver's Journal

"The trouble with you,
mister
is that you came over here
expecting to find
lumberjacks"

PYRITE

The man who first settled this area
came across the bar in a long-boat
and lived through the first rainy winter
in a hut fashioned in the bowels
of a big Western Red Cedar.

He must have traded with the Indians
who brought gold down from a secret
mine in these mtns of the Coast Range.

At Stone's Camp in a shake cabin
under dripping fir boughs I spent one
winter exploring, looking for that mine
and prospecting for gold in the streams.

My father always said you never find
gold unless it is in hard rock.
I found a woman
to walk the woods and river banks with:
Iron Pyrite, in these mountains
of shale.

THE SHINGLE WEAVER

From most anywhere in Tillamook County
you can see the landmark: Gold Peak.
Here, at its base, in Stone's Camp
the peak itself is not visible. Below the cabin
in the river my younger sister almost drowned and I,
too, the coward, almost. They once hung my father
by the waist with ropes from the bridge.
After a night over the mist and icy water
he was sober. Long winter nights I spent
here talking to my older sister and listening
to the water roaring under the bridge, the short wave
radio and the rain falling through the tall fir trees.
Here, on this island of trees saved from a fire
that burned everything else for miles around,
I found the muddy roads,
through trees and along the rivers. My second boat
—a thirty foot gill netter—I left here: smoke
curling up from red cedar through
the timber, blown by the southwest wind
away from the sea, at my back, behind me.
Across the bridge there is a road leading
up the mountain. At the end of the road
there is a logging landing overgrown by alders.
These mountains are plentiful:
Iron Pyrite and *quipus* of wire rope . . .

GRINDSTONE MTN

Out of breath on the summit,
looking toward the Pacific
Ocean thru the fog, I am
remembering the story of
how some industrious man
was on his way thru these mtns
from Portland to Tillamook,
pack-horses laden with
grindstones—sorely needed—at
that moment. Here he was met
by another man coming up
with the news that a ship
had arrived: Grindstones
were no longer needed
in Tillamook, so he dumped
all the stones down the slopes
of this mountain, where
I straddle the ridge.

CEDAR BUTTE LOOK-OUT: 1953

Once inside the cedar shake cabin
I quickly climb the ladder, hoping
always to make some discovery, to
see something new from that view
point in the small cupola.

During the first week of fire
I perform the ritual
of sweeping up the fallen, the dead
flying ants.

Pausing from my task, I see the fading
silhouettes of planes
tacked to the strips of window frame,
marking off dusty panes of glass
(Reminders of the 40's
and those unsuccessful Japanese
incendiary bombs, floating
on the west wind, devised
to catch in the arms of tall firs—

We are always finding them
in the woods: Japanese
lanterns rotting in the rain).

I see the ocean, to the West,
over snag covered ridge tops.

And the buzzard circling the cupola
is not among the aircraft on those cards.

FOR A MOUNTAIN GIRL

In early October
the Northern Lights
cover half the sky

— the end of the world

Salmonberry Guard Station
where the swift/clean Salmonberry
joins the muddy Nehalem . . .

the only thing that
has happened in three weeks

— the rest: eating, sleeping
and fishing or looking:
for the bleached dead
eels and suckers in the potholes

— Look-outs all along the ridges
of the Coast Range
report a huge fire burning

somewhere else.

You had come and (—we stood
together on the railroad
bridge over the swift river) gone

CRABBING AT NETARTS

Does the oyster remember
the grain of sand
that started it all?

Does the man
who found the oyster remember
which, among all the shells, was
the one opened with his knife . . .

& which man
does the sea remember?
Which man was it that fell
overboard and down and down and down
come up / went down?

Does the crab remember
where the flesh came from? I

lift the crab-pot dripping
sea-water onto the deck, take
out a crab, measure him,
throw him back into
the sea, keeping the rusty knife

saying to myself, I'll never forget
when and where I found that knife

CUTTING SHAKE-BOLTS ON THE EAST FORK

for the Old Man

We cut up a lot of big cedars
that winter, bucking them first into rounds
then, with a wedge and mall,
split them into rough bolts.
But it was only occasionally
in the narrow canyons
we found the slabs, the really good
cedar; they split easily and make
the best shingles and shakes.
For the big western red cedar
is hollow, partially, anyway
and when it falls, if its grain is straight,
breaks up long and thin.
I figure when old "Rip" falls
(though by then he will have forgotten
  all about that nickname and cedar)
he will splinter into about
six dozen long straight grained slabs.

FOUR THIRTY P.M.

. . . Quitting
Time: the rusting tin can
hung over the willow
limb by the spring
around the corner
on the way down
the dusty road
from Cedar Butte

Or the spike deer
we threw on the truck
For no reason
still,
warm,
bleeding
through the neck.

Taking his afternoon nap
perhaps dreaming of
those years

—of highball
logging with steam donkeys
pulling wrist thick
cables until they snap

and falling douglas fir
by hand, with the bullfiddle,
leaving stumps bigger around
than the table in the cookhouse
and smoother

—of silver rail-roads, the only
roads through the green virgin
timber stands

endless, the passing of the log
trains down the toothpick trestles

—of cork boots riddling
hard-wood dance floors
on Saturday night . . .

Through the window towards Gold Peak
dog-hair stands of buckskin snags:
white haze along the ridgetops

    Now a camp cook in summer
    too old to do timber cruising
    painting road signs of roads he pioneered

Snoozing in August afternoon, on the army cot,
snow haired, tale teller, old Tupper.

Trask Guard Station
Fire Season: 1952-53

THE BLACKSMITH SHOP AT ST LUKE

for my grandfather

The last
link

glowing orange,
is forged

on the point of
the anvil

& lies
at the bottom, half-

buried
in the sediment

of the
cooling

barrel (a union
carbide can)

No one seems
to remember

the splash & the
final

          sizzling
sound

1947

On winter
days when the pump is
frozen we have to carry water
a half mile further
from old Mr. Graham's
wishing well, its mossy wood
cover protects
the old
bucket,
squeaking pulley
frayed
wet rope, that makes callouses
on the hands
(the occasional dead
mouse we find, things
are generally ignored)
we draw
sweet water

ARE YOU SURE YOU ARE LYING TO ME?

It was not enough
to have found the ferns
in the fossils, the lumps of cheap coal
hidden under the bed to keep them
from being burned up in the pot bellied stove
by cold adults who did not appreciate
(it would have been impossible
to explain to them) that diamonds
& coal are one in the same
one of the substances infinitely older
like the parents who tell the child
go wash your hands, wash the coal dust
off your hands and come to supper

TRASK RIVER

July, 1955

over
slick
rocks
down
the
rapids
playing
until
we
had
gone
too
far
into
the
forty
foot
hole
under
the
bridge
and
realizing
she
could
not
swim
panicked
thrashing
her
arms
I
swimming
to
her
caught
in
death's
arms
too
almost

THE VALLEY BY TRASK HOUSE

I always imagined
it was here
that old Joe Champion
(after the first hard
  winter) crawled out
of his bark shanty
like a big black bear
to find himself
face to face with an Indian
    —Not sure if the Tillamook
      with his bow and arrow
      shot Champion, thinking
      the white man was a bear
      or thinking that he was
      Joe Champion and ought to be shot
      for trying to steal the gold
      brought down from the secret mine
Maybe Champion thought the Indian
was some kind of wild animal.
Both startled,
      maybe they shot
      each other

—This arrowhead
& several others.

THE KNOT

His dreams always had the scent
of cedar & pitch
bubbles in July not unlike the blisters
on his hands the first three weeks

work. Water from the rusty tin
cup at the spring beside
the road had its own taste, the animals
must have known that, the tear
drop shape of each half of the deer
tracks in the mud indicated
the popularity of that drinking

place. Spitting in the palm of his
hand extinguishing a cigarette
there a kind of concern for the woods

or lighting a cigarette in the 40 mph
wind, cupping his hands just so, drawing
once, just in the right way, a
skill, like rolling a smoke
on horseback, drawing the string
tight with the teeth on the pouch of
Bull Durham.

He had never done any of those
things, except, maybe, while
dreaming, instead he sharpened pencils,
unaware of the scent of cedar in

that. There is something in the smell
of wood, he thought, his life
somewhere in the grain
swirls of timber
bound log left behind;
like the eddies down be
low in the river. Red

the word of wood
he would think
about it or better
dream it all night.

The next day he would wake
fatigued, go out looking
for the log with that
pattern or after the rain walk
the river bank
looking at the swirls

saw instead the small fingerling
salmon caught in the pot
hole carved out of shale by the past
currents, caught sight of the red
crayfish, scurrying backward missing
one claw, frightened by the shadow

he gives it up, goes back to the city
finding no answers
in the past, uncertain
of the future

gives it all up
and searches in his dreams
for that pattern, that
swirl of light
around him like the grain of wood
flowing
around a knot

GHOSTS

Barney told me
at least once a week
"Don't get caught
 in the bite of the line"
(old logger's admonition
 in steam donkey highline
 logging).
While the logs were being yarded
to the tree one caught on a stump
and it was Barney
who hopped over the slack cable
to check the choker bell
just at the moment
it snapped tight —split
exactly
in half from the crotch
up. Barney: one
of the Murphy boys. Someone
went for his brother
who owned the company.
"Get back to work, you
 loggerhead sonofabitch," the brother
said, "We'll take him in tonight
when this train of logs is loaded."
Lying in the shade

of the water tank
he waits for the evening
log train to Carleton,
two halves
of a peeled alder log
turning red

CAULK BOOTS

I keep thinking
of that song:
"These boots wuz made for walkin . . . "
Fairly certain the old timers
would have liked that
especially the second line
of the chorus
as I watch the people
going in and coming out
of the Tillamook county courthouse
where the sign above the door
reads: "No Caulk Boots Allowed."
Great sport in the old days
loggers with a snoot full
invading the dance hall.
What twelve pairs of
caulk boots could do
to the hardwood dance floor
at South Prairie.
The smell of whale grease on
new boots
sawdust, saw-oil, mix
sweat, beer and hard
liquor. The floor
of the courthouse is marble.
On the lawn is the butt
of the biggest log ever
brought out of the Coast Range

SHATTERING OF A MYTH

My old man was
skinny and tall
How I teased him
locking him out, one day
sticking my tongue out
at him   made faces
through the window of
the door

never figuring
the drunk fist
could find my chin

knocking me flat
on my ass

w/out so much as
a scratch
to those boney knuckles

from all that
broken glass

I FEEL LIKE

My uncle on his way home from town
late one night, walking the tracks . . .
As he was crossing a trestle
he heard the train coming. He quick
hopped down and hung by his hands
from a railroad tie until the train had passed.
Not knowing how far his feet were from the ground
he hung there like that the rest of the night.
At daybreak he discovered his feet were exactly
four inches from the ground. It made him
so goddam mad
he hung there until sundown.

OREGON ASH

for Michael who knows not
Oregon Ash or railroad tracks

Big old Oregon Ash
outside
my window; creek
that used to come up
to the bottom of the
10 x 10 blocks (remembering
Kansas and the flood
brown waters of the Smoky Hill)
supporting my half of the shack.
Rain on the tarpaper;
wind through cracks in the ship-
lap; creek, gurgling;
green ash limb
whipping the siding, all
night as I
pretend this railroad shack
a ship
in the stormy dark
at sea;
that the creek
goes somewhere
further than the mill-
ponds where logs rot.

THE BARK SHANTY

I don't know if anyone ever saw
that bark shanty they named the road for.
I know the Railroad Grade used to be a railroad,
for the traffic of log trucks uncovers
those tracks that shine through boiling dust.
Once, to remove the water line, we spent days
digging up railroad ties: protection, sound
after thirty years. A few of the old toothpick
trestles stand, cross-hatch visible through
the second growth. As I drive up the Toll Road,
reaching for low-hole and praying
that no truck is coming down, it is easy to imagine
the stagecoach from Yamhill bouncing
over the rocky track, passengers
gritting teeth, hoping to see
the stage house just around the bend.
Down there below by the river
they know Trask House is waiting:
two or three lighted windows, rest
before traveling on to Tillamook.
This afternoon
I make the turns hold far to the outside
(just in case) and sound my horn. Further up
the spike deer lifts his head to look
before bouncing off
into blooming lupine

If I talk about Hollywood, Beverly Hills, Dog Patch
Trask Ranch, East Fork Camp and Timbuktu
you will understand, because you
as I did, lived and worked in those places.
The others will not, for they are thinking
of California, Al Capp and the Orient.
They do not know the Tillamook County
of the twenties, thirties, forties and fifties.
Or if they have heard those names
they will take out their maps and search
without finding and think me
just another name dropper. Or when they
drive through the Coast Range, they will find
rotting wood logs, a few snags, rusting tin cans.

Those names are on my map.
Fire, snow and rain have destroyed the signs
of man in these mountains.
In 1953 I searched for Timbuktu (it was on the
map then) and never found it.
Nor any gold or gold mines in a long winter
of prospecting and exploring.
The story of the secret Indian gold mines
(the Indian would bring his gold to Tillamook
to trade for salt and yardage) is historical
fact, but their location was never
determined by the white man.

But where is the Indian?
And you, too, Tupper. I suppose
you are dead by now. Certainly
the world at large
does not know you. In some file
under the "T's" there must be an entry
that reads: Milton Tupper
born 188-. Logger, timber cruiser, cook,
road builder, log scaler, road sign painter. Died
195-.
There is a reason I am writing
you. Last week in Hoquiam
I saw something: a steam donkey,
on new skids, its boiler
painted bright red . . .
I thought of you and knew
you would be interested (I didn't realize
there were any steam pots left).
The part about the red boiler you will laugh
at, wherever you are.

Yrs,

skip

p.s. This is a poem which will be in a book
called shingle weaver's journal. That will mean
much to you.
You will say you have a poem to tell *me*.
We will both laugh at that one.